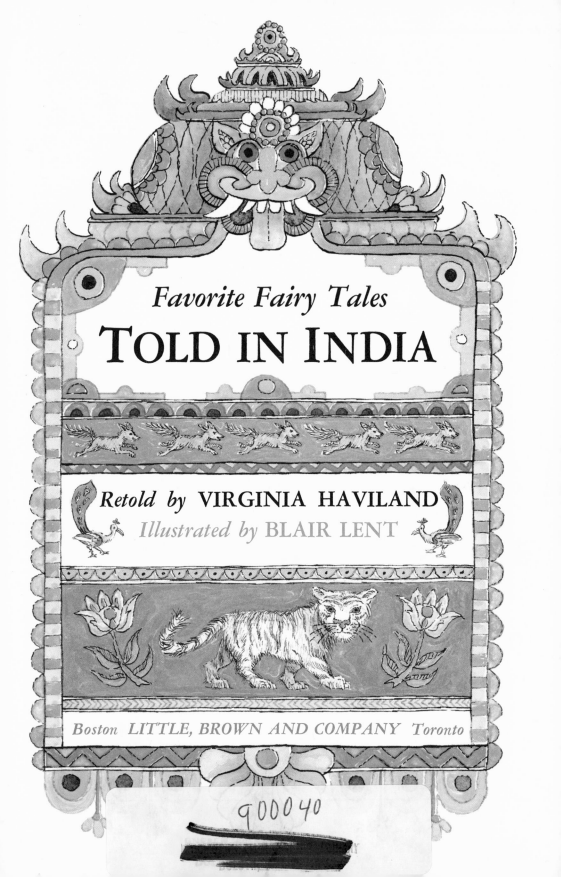

Favorite Fairy Tales
TOLD IN INDIA

Retold by VIRGINIA HAVILAND
Illustrated by BLAIR LENT

Boston LITTLE, BROWN AND COMPANY Toronto

Sources of the stories are as follows:

THE VALIANT CHATTEE-MAKER, THE LITTLE JACKALS AND THE LION, THE BLIND MAN, THE DEAF MAN, AND THE DONKEY, and THE ALLIGATOR AND THE JACKAL are retold from *Old Deccan Days; or, Hindoo Fairy Legends Current in Southern India,* collected in India by Mary E. Frere (Philadelphia, Lippincott, 1868).

THE CAT AND THE PARROT is retold with adaptation from *The Talking Thrush, Stories of Birds and Beasts,* collected in India by William Crooke (London, Dent, 1899).

SIR BUZZ is retold from Flora Annie Steel's *Tales of the Punjab* (London and New York, Macmillan, 1894).

THE TIGER, THE BRAHMAN, AND THE JACKAL is retold from *Indian Fairy Tales* by Joseph Jacobs (London and New York, Putnam, 1892).

THE BANYAN DEER is retold from *Tales of Jataka* by Ellen C. Babbitt. Copyright 1912, renewed 1940 by Ellen Babbitt. Reprinted by permission of the Century Company.

Library of Congress Cataloging in Publication Data

Haviland, Virginia, 1911–
    Favorite fairy tales told in India.

    CONTENTS: The valiant Chattee-maker.—The little
jackals and the lion.—The cat and the parrot. [etc.]
    1. Fairy tales. 2. Tales, Indic. [1. Fairy
tales. 2. Folklore—India] I. Lent, Blair, illus.
II. Title.
PZ8.H295Favg   398.2'0954   71-117019
ISBN 0-316-35055-9

Contents

The Valiant Chattee-Maker

ONCE UPON A TIME, in a violent storm of thunder, lightning, wind and rain, a tiger crept for shelter close to the wall of an old woman's hut. The old woman was very poor, and her hut but a tumbledown place. Through the roof the rain came drip, drip, drip everywhere. This troubled her so that she ran about from side to side, dragging first one thing and then another from under the leaks in the roof. As she did so she kept saying to herself, "Oh dear! Oh dear! How tiresome this is! I'm sure the roof will come down! If an elephant, or a lion, or a tiger were to walk in, he wouldn't frighten me half so much as does this perpetual dripping." And then she would drag the bed and all the other things in the room about again, to get them out of the way of the dripping water.

The tiger, crouching outside, heard all she said, and thought to himself, "This old woman says she would not be as afraid of an elephant, or a lion, or a tiger as she is of this perpetual dripping. What can this perpetual dripping be? It must be something very dreadful." And hearing her again dragging things about, he said to himself, "What a loud noise! Surely that must be the perpetual dripping."

At this moment a Chattee-maker, a maker of pots, came down the road in search of his straying donkey. The night being cold he had, truth to say, taken a little more toddy than was good for him and seeing, by the light of a flash of lightning, a large animal lying close to the old woman's hut, he mistook it for his donkey. Running up to the tiger, he seized it by one ear and began beating, kicking, and abusing it with all his might and main.

"You wretched creature!" he cried. "Is this the way you serve me, obliging me to come out and look for you in pouring rain and on such a dark night as this? Get up instantly, or I'll break every bone in your body." So he went on, scolding and thumping the tiger with all his strength, for he had worked himself up into a terrible rage.

The tiger did not know what to make of it all, but said to himself, "This must be the perpetual dripping. No wonder the old woman said she was more afraid of it than of an elephant, a lion, or a tiger. It gives most dreadfully hard blows."

The Chattee-maker, having made the tiger rise, got on his back and forced the beast to carry him home, kicking and beating the poor animal the whole way, all this time believing he was on his donkey. In front of his house he tied the tiger's forefeet and head together, and fastened him to a post. When he had done this he went to bed.

Next morning, when the Chattee-maker's wife got up and looked out of the window, what did she see but a great big tiger tied to their donkey's post. She was so surprised that she ran to awaken her husband, saying, "Do you know what animal you fetched home last night?"

"The donkey, to be sure," he answered.

"Come and look," said she, and she showed him the great tiger tied to the post. At this the Chattee-maker was no less astonished than his wife. He felt himself all over to see if the tiger had wounded him. No, he was safe and sound; and there was the tiger still fastened to the post.

News of the Chattee-maker's exploit soon spread through the village, and everyone came to see him and hear him tell how he had caught the tiger and tied it to a post. This they thought so

wonderful that they sent a deputation to the Rajah with a letter telling him how a man of their village, alone and unarmed, had caught a great tiger and tied it to a post.

When the Rajah read the letter he also was surprised. He determined to go in person to see so astonishing a sight. He sent for his horses and carriages, his lords and attendants, and off they all went to look at the Chattee-maker and the tiger he had caught.

Now the tiger was a very large one, and had long been the terror of the country around, which made the whole matter still more extraordinary. The Rajah decided to bestow all possible honor on the valiant Chattee-maker. He gave him houses and lands, and as much money as would fill a well. He made him a lord in his court, and conferred on him the command of ten thousand horses.

It came to pass, shortly after this, that a neighboring Rajah, who had long had a quarrel with this one, announced his intention to go to war with him. It was learned that this foreign Rajah had gathered a great army on the borders, and was prepared to invade the country.

No one knew what to do. The Rajah inquired of all his generals which one would be willing to take command of his forces to oppose the enemy. They all replied that the country was too ill-prepared. The cause was so hopeless that they did not wish to take the responsibility of chief command. The Rajah did not know whom he could appoint until some of his people said, "You have lately given the command of ten thousand horse to the valiant Chattee-maker who caught the tiger. Why not make him commander in chief? A man who could catch a tiger and tie him to a post must surely be more courageous and clever than most."

"Very well," said the Rajah, "I will make him commander in chief." So he sent for the Chattee-maker and said to him, "In your hands I place all the power of the kingdom. You must put our enemies to flight."

"So be it," answered the Chattee-maker. "But before I lead the whole army against the enemy, allow me to go by myself and examine their position and, if possible, find out their numbers and strength."

The Rajah consented. The Chattee-maker returned home and said to his wife, "The Rajah has made me commander in chief of his forces. It is a very difficult post for me to fill, because I shall have to ride at the head of the army, and you know that I have never in my life been on a horse. But I have succeeded in gaining a little delay. The Rajah has given me permission to go first alone and examine the enemy's camp. Get me a very quiet pony, for you know I cannot ride, and I will start tomorrow morning."

But before the Chattee-maker left, the Rajah sent over a most magnificent charger richly bedecked for him to ride when going to see the enemy's camp.

The Chattee-maker was frightened indeed, for

this great steed was powerful and spirited. He felt sure that even if he were able to get on it, he would very soon tumble off. But he did not dare to refuse it, lest he offend the Rajah. So he sent back to him a message of thanks, and said to his wife, "I cannot go on the pony, now that the Rajah has sent me this fine horse; but however am I to ride it?"

"Oh, don't be frightened," she answered. "You've only got to get up on it. I will tie you on firmly, so that you cannot tumble off. If you start at night, no one will see that you are tied on."

"Very well," he replied.

That night the Chattee-maker's wife brought to the door the horse that the Rajah had sent. "Indeed," said the Chattee-maker, "I can never get into that saddle. It is so high up."

"You must jump," said his wife. So several times the Chattee-maker tried to jump, but each time he tumbled down again. "I always forget when I am jumping," said he, "which way I ought to turn."

"Your face must be toward the horse's head," she answered.

"To be sure, of course!" he cried, and giving one great leap he jumped into the saddle, but with his face toward the horse's tail.

"This won't do at all," said his wife as she helped him down again. "Try getting on without jumping."

"I never can remember," he said, "when I have got my left foot in the stirrup, what to do with my right foot or where to put it."

"That must go in the other stirrup," she answered. "Let me help you."

Since the horse was fresh and lively and did not like standing still, it took many trials and many tumbles before the Chattee-maker got into the saddle. And no sooner had he got there than he cried, "Oh, wife, wife! Tie me very firmly as quickly as possible, for I know I shall jump down if I can."

The Chattee-maker's wife quickly fetched some strong rope and tied his feet firmly into the stirrups. She fastened one stirrup to the other, and put another rope round his waist and another round his neck, and fastened them all to the horse's body and neck and tail.

When the horse felt all these ropes about him he could not imagine what queer creature had got upon his back, and he began rearing and kicking and prancing. At last he set off at full gallop, as fast as he could tear, right across country.

"Wife, wife!" cried the Chattee-maker, "you forgot to tie my hands."

"Hold on by the mane!" she shouted after him. So he caught hold of the horse's mane as firmly as he could. Then away went horse, away went Chattee-maker — away, away, away, over hedges, over ditches, over rivers, over plains — away, away, like a flash of lightning — now this way, now that

— on, on, on, gallop, gallop, gallop — until they came in sight of the enemy's camp.

The Chattee-maker did not like his ride at all, and when he saw where it was leading him he liked it still less, for he thought the enemy would catch him and very likely kill him. He determined to make one desperate effort to be free. He stretched out his hand and seized a large banyan tree as he galloped past. He held on with all his might, hoping that this action would cause his ropes to break. But the horse was going so fast, and the soil in which the banyan tree grew was so loose, that when the Chattee-maker caught hold of the tree and gave it a violent pull it came up by the roots, and on he rode as fast as before, with the tree in his hand.

All the soldiers in the camp saw him coming. Having heard that an army was to be sent against them, they imagined that the Chattee-maker was the one in the lead. "See," they cried, "here comes a man of gigantic stature on a mighty horse! He is

one of the enemy. The whole army must be close at hand. If they are such as he, we are all dead men."

Running to their Rajah, the soldiers cried, "Here comes the whole force of the enemy. They are men of gigantic stature, mounted on mighty horses. As they come, they tear up the very trees in their rage. We can oppose men, but not such monsters as these." Other soldiers followed and said, "It is true," for by this time the Chattee-maker had got near the camp. "They are coming! They are coming! Let us fly! Let us fly! Fly! Fly, for your lives!"

The panic-stricken multitude fled from the camp. They had their Rajah write a letter to the one whose country he was about to invade to say that he would not do so, and to propose peace.

Scarcely had everyone fled from the camp when the horse on which the Chattee-maker rode came galloping into it. The Chattee-maker was almost dead from fatigue, but the banyan tree was still in his hand. Just as he reached the camp the ropes by which he was tied broke and let him fall to the ground. The horse stood still, too tired with his long run to go farther.

On recovering his senses, the Chattee-maker found to his surprise that the whole camp, full of rich arms, clothes and trappings, was entirely deserted. In the royal tent, moreover, he found a letter addressed to his Rajah, announcing the retreat of the invading army and proposing terms of peace.

The Chattee-maker took the letter and returned home with it as fast as he could, leading his horse all the way, for he was afraid to mount him again. By the direct road he reached home just before nightfall. His wife ran out to meet him, overjoyed at his speedy return. As soon as he saw her he said, "Ah, wife, since last I saw you I've been all around the world, and had many wonderful and terrible adventures. But never mind that now. Send this letter quickly to the Rajah, and the horse also. Since the horse looks so tired, the Rajah will see what a long ride I've had. By sending it ahead, I shall not be obliged to ride it up to the palace tomorrow morning and most likely tumble off."

The next day the Chattee-maker went to the palace. When the people saw him, they cried, "This man is as modest as he is brave. After putting our enemies to flight, he walks quite simply to the door instead of riding here in state as another man would."

The Rajah came to the palace door to meet the Chattee-maker, and paid him all possible honor. Terms of peace were agreed upon between the two countries, and the Chattee-maker was rewarded for all he had done with twice as much rank and wealth as he had had before. And he lived very happily all the rest of his life.

As for the tiger who had started him on his way to success, he came to the usual end of captured tigers.

The Little Jackals and the Lion

ONCE THERE WAS a great lion who was king of a great jungle. Whenever he wanted anything to eat, all he had to do was to come out of his cave and *roar*. A few roars so frightened the smaller creatures that they came out of their holes and hiding places and ran this way and that to get away. Then, of course, the lion could see them. He pounced on them, killed them, and gobbled them up at once.

The lion did this so often that at last not a creature was left alive in the jungle except the lion himself and two little jackals who were mates.

The two jackals had run away from the lion so many times that they were now thin and tired and could not run fast any more. One day the lion came so near to their heels that the little mother jackal cried, "Oh, Father Jackal, Father Jackal! The lion is going to catch us this time!"

"Pooh! Nonsense, Mother!" said the little father jackal. "Come, we can run a bit faster!"

So they ran, ran, ran faster, and the lion did not catch them this time.

But at last came a day when the lion was so near that the little mother jackal was even more frightened.

"Oh, Father Jackal, Father Jackal!" she cried. "The lion will eat us this time."

"No, Mother, don't you fret," said the little father jackal. "Do just as I tell you, and all will be well."

What did those cunning little jackals do now but take hands and run towards the lion — as if they had intended to do this from the first. When the lion saw them coming he stood up, and he roared in his terrible voice, "You miserable little wretches, come here and be eaten, at once! Why didn't you come before?"

The father jackal bowed very low.

"Indeed, Father Lion," he said, "we meant to

come before. We know we ought to have come before. And we wanted to come before. But every time we started to come, a dreadful great lion came out of the woods and roared at us, and frightened us so that we ran away."

"What do you mean?" roared the lion. "There's no other lion in this jungle, and you know it!"

"Indeed, indeed, Father Lion," said the little jackal. "I know that is what everybody thinks. But indeed and indeed there is another lion! And he is as much bigger than you as you are bigger than I! His face is much more terrible, and his roar far, far more dreadful. Oh, he is far more fearful than you!"

At that the lion stood up and roared so that the jungle shook.

"Take me to this lion," he said. "I'll eat him up and then I'll eat you up."

The little jackals danced on ahead, and the lion stalked behind. They led him to a place where there was a round, deep well of clear water. They went around one side of it, and the lion stalked up to the other.

"He lives down there, Father Lion!" said the little jackal. "He lives down there!"

The lion came close and looked down into the water. And a lion's face looked back at him out of the water!

When he saw that, the lion roared and shook his mane and showed his teeth. And the lion in the water shook his mane and showed his teeth. The lion above shook his mane again and growled again, and made a terrible face. But the lion in the

water made just as terrible a face. The lion above could not stand that. He leaped down into the well after the other lion.

Of course, as you know very well, there wasn't any other lion! It was only the reflection in the water!

So the poor old lion floundered about and floundered about, but he couldn't get up the steep sides of the well, so he was drowned. And when he was dead the little Jackals took hands and danced round the well, and sang:

> "*The lion is dead! The lion is dead!*
> *We have killed the great lion who would*
>   *have killed us!*
> *The lion is dead! The lion is dead!*
> *Ao! Ao! Ao!*"

The Cat and the Parrot

ONCE UPON A TIME a cat and a parrot agreed
to ask each other to dinner in turn. First the cat
would ask the parrot, then the parrot would invite
the cat, and so on.

The cat in his turn was so stingy that he provided nothing for dinner but a pint of milk, a
small slice of fish, and a bit of rice — which the
parrot had to cook himself! He was too polite to
complain, but he did not find it a good meal.

When it was the parrot's turn to entertain the
cat, he cooked a great dinner, and did it before his
guest arrived. Most tempting of all he offered was
a clothes-basketful of crisp, brown cakes. He put
four hundred and ninety-eight spicy cakes before
the cat, and kept only two for himself.

Well, the cat ate every bit of the good food
prepared by the parrot and began on the pile of

cakes. He ate the four hundred and ninety-eight, then asked for more.

"Here are my two cakes," said the parrot. "You may eat them."

The cat ate the two cakes. He then looked around and asked for still more.

"Well," said the parrot, "I don't see anything more, unless you wish to eat me!"

The cat showed no shame. Slip! Slop! Down his throat went the parrot!

An old woman who happened to be near saw all this and threw a stone at the cat. "How dreadful to eat your friend the parrot!"

"Parrot, indeed!" said the cat. "What's a parrot? I've a great mind to eat you, too." And before you could say a word, slip! slop! down went the old woman!

The cat started down the road, feeling fine. Soon he met a man driving a donkey. When the man saw the cat he said, "Run away, cat, or my donkey might kick you to death."

"Donkey, indeed!" said the cat. "I have eaten five hundred cakes, I've eaten my friend the parrot, I've eaten an old woman. What's to keep me from eating an old man and a donkey?" Slip! Slop! Down went the old man and the donkey.

The cat next met the wedding procession of a king. Behind the king and his new bride marched a column of soldiers and behind them a row of elephants, two by two. The king said to the cat, "Run away, cat, or my elephants might trample you to death."

"Ho!" said the cat. "I've eaten five hundred cakes, I've eaten my friend the parrot, I've eaten an old woman, I've eaten an old man and a donkey. What's to keep me from eating a beggarly king?"

Slip! Slop! Down went the king, the queen, the soldiers, and all the elephants!

The cat went on until he met two land crabs,

scuttling along in the dusk. "Run away, cat," they squeaked, "or we will nip you!"

"Ho! Ho! Ho!" laughed the cat, shaking his fat sides. "I've eaten five hundred cakes, I've eaten my friend the parrot, I've eaten an old woman, I've eaten an old man with a donkey, I've eaten a king and a queen, his soldiers, and all his elephants. Shall I run away from land crabs? No. I'll eat you, too!"

Slip! Slop! Down went the land crabs.

When the land crabs got down inside the cat, they found themselves among a crowd of creatures. They could see the unhappy king with his bride, who had fainted. The soldiers were trying

to march, and the elephants trumpeted while the donkey brayed as the old man beat it. The old woman and the parrot were there, and last of all, the five hundred cakes neatly piled in a corner.

The land crabs ran around to see what they could do. "Let's nip!" they said. So, nip! nip! nip! they made a round hole in the side of the cat. Nip! nip! nip! until the hole was big enough to let them all walk through. The land crabs scuttled out and away. Then out walked the king, carrying his bride; out walked the soldiers and the elephants, two by two; out walked the old man, driving his donkey; out walked the old woman, giving the cat a piece of her mind; and last of all, out walked the parrot with a cake in each claw!

The Blind Man, the Deaf Man, and the Donkey

A BLIND MAN AND A DEAF MAN once entered into partnership. The deaf man was to see for the blind man, and the blind man was to hear for the deaf man.

One day they went together to a nautch — a musical and dancing entertainment. The deaf man said, "The dancing is very good, but the music is not worth listening to."

Whereupon the blind man said, "On the contrary, I think the music very good, but the dancing not worth looking at."

After this they went together for a walk in the jungle. There they found a donkey that had strayed away from its owner, carrying a great chattee such as clothes are boiled in.

The deaf man said to the blind man, "Brother, here are a donkey and a great big chattee, with nobody to own them! Let us take them with us; they may be useful to us some day."

"Very well," said the blind man, nodding his head, "we will take them with us."

So the blind man and the deaf man went on their way, taking the donkey and the great big chattee with them. A little farther on they came to an ants' nest, and the deaf man said to the blind man, "Here are a number of very fine black ants, much larger than any I ever saw before. Let us take some of them home to show to our friends."

"Very well," nodded the blind man. "We will take them as a present to our friends." So the deaf man took a silver snuffbox out of his pocket, and put four or five of the finest black ants into it. They then continued on their journey.

Before they had gone far, a terrible storm came up. It thundered and lightninged and rained and blew with such fury that it seemed as if heaven and earth were at war.

"Oh dear! Oh dear!" cried the deaf man. "How

dreadful this lightning is! Let us make haste and get to shelter."

"I don't see that the lightning is dreadful at all," answered the blind man, "but the thunder is very terrible. We must certainly seek some place of shelter."

Not far off they came to a high building which looked to the deaf man like a fine temple. He and the blind man resolved to spend the night there. They went inside and shut the door, taking the donkey and the big chattee with them.

But this building, which they mistook for a temple, was in truth no temple at all but the house of a powerful Rakshasa, or demon. Hardly had the blind man, the deaf man and the donkey got inside and fastened the door than the Rakshasa returned home. He found the door fastened and heard people moving about inside.

"Ho! ho!" he said to himself. "Some men have got in here, have they! I'll soon make mincemeat out of them." So he began to roar in a voice louder than the thunder, and he shouted, "Let me into my house this minute, you wretches! Let me in, let me in, I say!" He kicked the door and battered it with his great fists.

Though the Rakshasa's voice was powerful, his appearance was still more alarming. The deaf man, peeping at him through a chink in the wall, was so frightened that he did not know what to do. But the blind man was brave, because he couldn't see. He went to the door and called out, "Who are you? And what do you mean by battering at the door this way at this time of night?"

"I'm a Rakshasa," answered the Rakshasa angrily, "and this is my house. Let me in this instant, or I'll kill you."

All this time the deaf man, watching the Rakshasa, was shivering and shaking, but the blind man was still very brave and he called out again, "Oh, you're a Rakshasa, are you! Well, if you're Rakshasa, I'm Bakshasa. And Bakshasa is as good as Rakshasa!"

"Bakshasa!" roared the Rakshasa. "Bakshasa! Bakshasa! What nonsense is this? There is no such creature as a Bakshasa!"

"Go away," replied the blind man, "and don't dare to make any further disturbance, lest I punish you. Know that I'm Bakshasa! And Bakshasa is Rakshasa's father!"

"My father?" answered the Rakshasa. "Heaven and earth! Bakshasa, my father! I never heard anything so extraordinary. You, my father, and in there! I never knew my father was Bakshasa."

"Yes," replied the blind man. "Go away instantly, I command you, for I am your father Bakshasa."

"Very well," answered the Rakshasa, beginning to be puzzled. "But if you're my father, let me first see your face."

The blind man and the deaf man were unsure what they should do now, but at last they opened the door a tiny chink and poked the donkey's nose out.

When the Rakshasa saw this, he thought to himself, "Bless me, what a terribly ugly face my father Bakshasa has!" Then he called out, "O Father Bakshasa, you have a very big, fierce face, but people sometimes have very big heads and very little bodies. Pray let me see your body as well as your head before I go away."

The blind man and the deaf man now rolled the great, big chattee with a thundering noise past the chink in the door.

The Rakshasa, watching attentively, was very surprised when he saw this great black thing rolling along the floor, and he thought, "In truth, my father Bakshasa has a very big body as well as a big head. He's big enough to eat me up altogether. I'd better go away." Still he could not help being a little doubtful, so he cried, "O Bakshasa, Father

Bakshasa! You have indeed got a very big head and a very big body. But do, before I go away, let me hear you scream."

The cunning deaf man, seeing what the Rakshasa said, pulled his silver snuffbox out of his pocket. He took out the black ants, put one in the donkey's right ear, another in the donkey's left ear, and another and another. The ants pinched the poor donkey's ears dreadfully. The donkey was so hurt and frightened that it began to bellow, "Eh augh! Eh augh! Eh augh! Augh! Augh!"

At this terrible noise, the Rakshasa fled in fright, saying, "Enough, enough, Father Bakshasa! The sound of your voice would make the most obstinate Rakshasa obedient."

No sooner had he gone than the deaf man took the ants out of the donkey's ears, and he and the blind man spent the rest of the night in peace and comfort.

Next morning the deaf man woke the blind man early, saying, "Awake, brother, awake. Here we are in great luck. The floor is covered with heaps of gold and silver and precious stones."

"That is a good thing," said the blind man. "Show me where it is so I can help you collect it." They collected as much treasure as they could manage and made four great bundles of it. The blind man took one bundle, the deaf man took another, and putting the other two great bundles on the donkey, they started off home.

However, the Rakshasa whom they had frightened away the night before had not gone very far. He was waiting to see what his father Bakshasa might look like by day. He saw the door of his house open and watched while out walked—a blind man, a deaf man, and a donkey, all of them laden with large bundles of his treasure.

The Rakshasa, in a rage, called to six of his friends to help him kill the blind man, the deaf man and the donkey, and recover the treasure.

The deaf man saw them coming — seven great Rakshasas, with hair a yard long and tusks like an elephant's. He was terrified, but the blind man, still very brave, said, "Brother, why do you lag behind in that way?"

"Oh!" cried the deaf man, "there are seven great Rakshasas with tusks like an elephant's coming to kill us. What can we do?"

"Let us hide the treasure in the bushes," said the blind man, pointing. "And you lead me to a tree. I will climb up first, and you shall climb up afterward. Thus we shall be out of their way." So they

pushed the donkey and the bundles of treasure into
the bushes, and the deaf man led the blind man to
a high tree close by. But he was a very cunning man
and instead of letting the blind man climb up first,
he got up first and let the blind man follow, so
that he was farther out of harm's way than his
friend.

When the Rakshasa arrived at the place and saw
them both perched out of reach in the tree, he said
to his friends, "Let us get on each other's shoul-

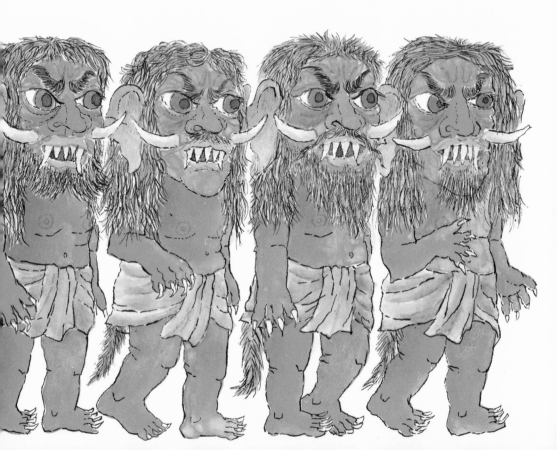

ders. We shall then be high enough to pull them down." So one Rakshasa stooped down, and the second got on his shoulders, and the third on his, and the fourth on his, and the fifth on his, and the sixth on his. The seventh and last Rakshasa got on top.

The deaf man became so frightened that he caught hold of his friend's arm, crying, "They're coming, they're coming!" The blind man was not in a very secure position, sitting carelessly at his ease, not knowing how close the Rakshasas were. Thus when the deaf man gave him this unexpected push, he lost his balance and tumbled down onto the neck of the seventh Rakshasa.

The blind man had no idea where he was, but thought he had got onto the branch of some other tree. Stretching out his hand for something to catch hold of, he caught hold of the Rakshasa's two great ears, and pinched them hard in his surprise and fright. With the pain and the weight of the blind man the Rakshasa lost his balance and fell to the ground, knocking down in turn the sixth, fifth, fourth, third, second, and first Rakshasas, who rolled over one another and lay in a confused heap at the foot of the tree.

Meanwhile the blind man called out to his friend, "Where am I? What has happened? Where am I? Where am I?"

The deaf man, safe up in the tree, called, "Well done, brother! Never fear! Never fear! You're all right, only hold on tight. I'm coming down to help you."

The deaf man had not the least intention of leaving his place of safety, but he continued to call out, "Never mind, brother. Hold on as tight as you can. I'm coming, I'm coming." The more he yelled, the harder the blind man pinched the Rakshasa's ears, which he mistook for palm branches.

The other six Rakshasas who, after a good deal of kicking, had succeeded in pulling themselves from their tangled heap, had had quite enough

of helping their friend, so they ran away as fast as they could.

The seventh Rakshasa thought from their going that the danger must be greater than he knew. Being, moreover, very much afraid of the creature that sat on his shoulders, he put his hands to the back of his ears, and pushed off the blind man. Then, without staying to see who or what it was, he ran after his six companions as fast as he could.

As soon as all the Rakshasas were out of sight, the deaf man came down from the tree and picking up the blind man, embraced him, saying, "I could not have done better myself. You have frightened away all our enemies." He then dragged the donkey and the bundles of treasure out of the bushes, gave the blind man one bundle to carry, took the second himself, and put the remaining two on the donkey, as before. This done, the whole party set off to return home. But when they had got nearly out of the jungle, the deaf man suggested that they divide the treasure.

"Very well," nodded the blind man. "Divide what we have in the bundles into two equal portions, keeping one half yourself and giving me the other."

The cunning deaf man had no intention of giving up half of the treasure to the blind man. First he took his own bundle of treasure and hid it in the bushes, and then he took the two bundles off the donkey and hid them in the bushes, and he took a good deal of treasure out of the blind man's bundle, which he also hid. Then, taking the small quantity that remained, he divided it into two equal portions, placing half before the blind man and half in front of himself.

When the blind man put out his hand and felt the very little heap of treasure he became angry and cried, "This is not fair. You are deceiving me. You have kept almost all the treasure for yourself and given me only a very little."

"Oh, oh! How can you be angry?" said the deaf man. "If you do not believe me, feel for yourself.

See, my heap of treasure is no larger than yours."

The blind man put out his hands again to feel how much his friend had kept. When he found that in front of the deaf man lay only a very small heap, no larger than what he had himself received, he got very cross, and said, "Come, come, this won't do. You think you can cheat me in this way because I am blind. But I'm not so stupid as all that. I carried a great bundle of treasure. You carried a great bundle of treasure. And there were two great bundles on the donkey. Do you mean to pretend that all that made no more treasure than these two little heaps? No, indeed. I know better than that."

"Stuff and nonsense!" said the deaf man.

"Stuff or no stuff," continued the other, "you are trying to take me in, and I won't be taken in by you."

And so they went on bickering, scolding, growling, contradicting until the blind man got so enraged that he gave the deaf man a tremendous box on the ear.

The blow was so violent that it made the deaf man hear!

The deaf man, very angry, gave his neighbor in return so hard a blow in the face that it opened the blind man's eyes!

The deaf man could hear as well as see! And the blind man could see as well as hear! This astounded them both so much that they became good friends again. The deaf man confessed to having hidden the bulk of the treasure, which he thereupon dragged forth from its place of concealment, and having divided it equally, they went home and enjoyed themselves.

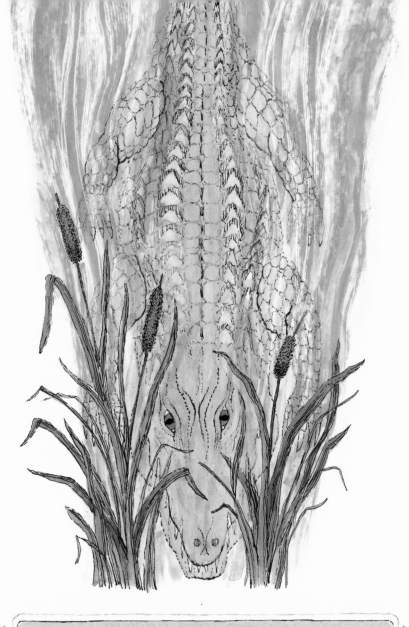

The Alligator and the Jackal

A HUNGRY JACKAL once went down to a river in search of little crabs and whatever else he could find for his dinner. Now it chanced that in this river there lived a big alligator who, being also very hungry, would have been glad to eat the jackal.

The jackal ran up and down, looking here and there, but for a long time could find nothing to eat. At last, near the alligator, who was lying in the clear, shallow water among some tall bulrushes, he saw a little crab sidling along as fast as his legs could carry him. The jackal was so hungry that too quickly he tried to catch the crab, and snap! the old alligator caught hold of *him*.

"Oh dear!" thought the jackal to himself. "What can I do? In another minute this great alligator will drag me down under the water and kill me. I must make him think he has made a mistake."

In a cheerful voice the jackal called out, "Clever alligator, clever alligator, to catch hold of a bulrush root instead of my paw! I hope you will find it tender."

The alligator, so deep in bulrushes that he could hardly see, thought, "Dear me, how tiresome! I fancied I had caught hold of the jackal's paw, but there he is calling out." He let the jackal go.

The jackal ran away as fast as he could, crying, "O wise alligator, wise alligator! So you let me go again!"

The alligator was very much vexed, but the jackal had run too far away to be caught.

Next day as usual the jackal returned to the river to get his dinner, but this time, not seeing the alligator, he called out, "When I go to look for my dinner, I see little crabs peeping through the mud; then I catch them and eat them. I wish I could see one now."

The alligator, who was buried in the mud at the bottom of the river, heard every word. Up he popped the point of his snout, thinking, "If I do but show just the tip of my nose, the jackal will take me for a crab and put in his paw to catch me. As soon as he does, I'll gobble him up."

But no sooner did the jackal see the little tip of the alligator's nose than he called out, "Aha, my friend! There you are. No dinner for me today in this part of the river." So saying, he ran on and fished for his dinner a long way off.

The alligator was angry at missing his prey a second time, and determined not to let him escape again.

So the following day, when his little tormentor returned to the river, the alligator hid close to the bank, to catch him if he could.

Now the jackal was rather afraid of going near the water. But, being hungry, he cried, "Where are all the little crabs? Generally, even when they are under water, I can see that they are blowing *bubble, bubble, bubble,* and all the little bubbles go *pop! pop! pop!"*

The alligator, who was buried in the mud under the river bank thought, "I will pretend to be a little crab." He began to blow, *"Puff, puff, puff! Bubble, bubble, bubble!"* All the great bubbles rushed to the surface of the river and burst there, and the waters eddied round and round like a whirlpool. There was such a commotion when the huge monster blew bubbles that the jackal saw very well who must be there. He ran away as fast as he could, saying, "Thank you, kind alligator, thank you, thank you! Indeed, I would not have come here had I known you were so close."

This enraged the alligator. To himself he said, "I will be taken in no more. Next time I will be very cunning." For a long time the alligator waited for the jackal to return.

But the jackal did not come, for he had thought to himself, "If matters go on in this way, I shall some day be caught and eaten by the wicked old alligator. I had better content myself with living on wild figs." He went no more near the river, but stayed in the jungle and ate wild figs and roots.

When the alligator found this out, he determined to try and catch the jackal on land. Going to the largest of the wild fig trees, where the ground was covered with fallen fruit, he collected a quantity of it. Burying himself under the great heap, he waited for the jackal to appear. But no sooner did the cunning little animal see this great heap of wild figs than he thought, "That looks very like my friend the alligator." To discover if it were so, he called out, "The juicy little wild figs I love to eat always tumble down from the tree, and roll here and there as the wind drives them. This great heap of figs is quite still. These cannot be good figs. I will not eat any of them."

"Ho, ho!" thought the alligator, "is that all? How suspicious this jackal is! I will make the figs roll about a little, and when he sees that, he will come and eat them."

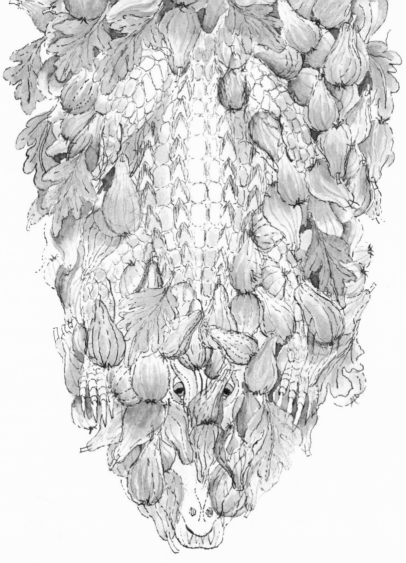

So the great beast shook himself, and all the little figs went roll, roll, roll, this way and that way, farther than they had ever rolled before and beyond where the most blustering wind could have driven them.

Seeing this, the jackal scampered away, saying, "I am so much obliged to you, alligator, for letting me know you are there, for indeed I should hardly have guessed it. You were so buried under that heap of figs."

The alligator was so angry that he ran after the jackal, but the latter ran away too quickly to be caught.

Now the alligator said to himself, "I will not allow that little wretch to make fun of me another time. I will show him that I can be more cunning than he fancies."

Early the next morning the alligator crawled as fast as he could to the jackal's den, a hole in the side of a hill. He crept into it and hid, waiting for the jackal, who was out, to return home.

When the jackal got near his hole, he looked about and thought, "Dear me! The ground looks as if some heavy creature has been dragging over it. And here are great clods of earth knocked down from each side of my den. A very big animal must have been trying to squeeze through the door. I certainly will not go inside until I know that all is safe in there." So he called out, "Little house, pretty house, my sweet little house, why do you not answer when I call? When I come home and all is safe and right, you always call out to me. Is anything wrong, that you do not speak?"

The alligator inside thought, "If that is the case I had better call out, that he may fancy all is right in his house." In as gentle a voice as he could find, he said, "Sweet little jackal."

The jackal now felt afraid. He thought to himself, "So the dreadful old alligator is here. I must try to kill him if I can, for if I do not he will certainly kill me." He answered at once, "Thank you, my dear little house. I am glad to hear your pretty voice. In a minute I shall come in, but first I must collect firewood to cook my dinner."

Off he ran as fast as he could, and dragged all the dry branches and bits of sticks he could find up to the mouth of the den.

The alligator inside kept quiet, but he could not help laughing a little to himself as he thought, "So at last I have deceived this tiresome little jackal. In a few minutes he will run in, and then won't I snap him up!"

When the jackal had gathered together all the sticks he could find and had arranged them around the mouth of his den, he set them on fire and pushed them into his hole. He had such a quantity of wood that it soon blazed up into a great fire, and the smoke and flames filled the den. The fire quickly smothered the wicked old alligator and then burned him to death.

Outside, the little jackal ran up and down dancing for joy and singing, "How do you like my house, my friend? Is it nice and warm? Dingdong! Ding-dong! The alligator is dying! Dingdong! Ding-dong! He will trouble me no more. I have defeated my enemy! Ring-a-ting! Ding-a-ting! Ding-ding-dong!"

Sir Buzz

ONCE UPON A TIME a soldier died leaving a widow and one son. They were very poor, and at last matters became so bad that they had nothing left in the house to eat.

"Mother," said the son, "give me four shillings, and I will go seek my fortune in the wide world."

"Alas!" answered the mother. "And where am I, who haven't a farthing wherewith to buy bread, to find four shillings?"

"There is that old coat of my father's," returned the lad. "Look in the pocket — perchance there is something there."

So she looked, and behold! There were six shillings hidden away at the very bottom of the pocket.

"More than I bargained for," said the lad, laughing. "See, Mother, these two shillings are for you;

you can live on that till I return. The rest will pay my way until I find my fortune."

So he set off to find his fortune, and on the way he saw a tigress, licking her paw, and moaning mournfully. He was just about to run away from the dangerous creature when she called to him faintly, saying, "Good lad, if you will take out this thorn, I shall be forever grateful."

"Not I!" answered the lad. "If I begin to pull it out, and it pains you, you will kill me with a pat of your paw."

"No, no!" cried the tigress. "I will turn my face to this tree, and when the pain comes I will pat *it*."

To this the soldier's son agreed; so he pulled out the thorn, and when the pain came the tigress gave the tree such a blow that the trunk split all to pieces. Then she turned towards the soldier's son and said gratefully, "Take this box as a reward, my son, but do not open it until you have traveled nine miles."

So the soldier's son thanked the tigress, and set

off with the box to find his fortune. When he had gone five miles, he felt certain that the box weighed more than it had at first, and with every step he took it seemed to grow heavier and heavier. He tried to struggle on—though it was all he could do to carry the box—until he had gone about eight miles and a quarter. Then his patience gave way.

"I believe that tigress was a witch, and is playing her tricks on me," he cried. "But I will stand this nonsense no longer. Lie there, you wretched box! Heaven knows what is in you, and I don't care."

So saying, he flung the box down on the ground. It burst open with the shock, and out stepped a little old man. He stood only one span high, but his beard was a span and a quarter long, and trailed upon the ground.

The little manikin immediately began to stamp about and scold the lad roundly for letting the box down so violently.

"Upon my word!" said the soldier's son, trying not to smile at the ridiculous little figure, "but you are weighty for your size, old gentleman! And what may your name be?"

"Sir Buzz!" snapped the one-span manikin, still stamping about in a great rage.

"Upon my word!" said the soldier's son once more. "If *you* are all the box contained, I am glad I didn't trouble to carry it farther."

"That's not polite," snarled the manikin. "Perhaps if you had carried it the full nine miles you might have found something better. But that's neither here nor there. I'm good enough for you, at any rate, and will serve you faithfully according to my mistress's orders."

"Serve me! Then I wish to goodness you'd serve me with some dinner, for I am mighty hungry. Here are four shillings to pay for it."

No sooner had the soldier's son said this and given the money, than with a *whiz! boom! bing!* like a big bee, Sir Buzz flew through the air to a confectioner's shop in the nearest town. There he stood, the one-span manikin, with the span-and-a-quarter beard trailing on the ground, by the big preserving pan, and cried in ever so loud a voice, "Ho! ho! Sir Confectioner, bring me some sweets!"

The confectioner looked round the shop, and out of the door, and down the street, but could see no one, for tiny Sir Buzz was quite hidden by the preserving pan. Then the manikin called out louder still, "Ho! ho! Sir Confectioner, bring me sweets!" And when the confectioner looked in vain for his customer, Sir Buzz grew angry, and ran and pinched him on the legs, and kicked him on the foot, saying, "Impudent knave! Do you mean to say you can't see *me*? Why, I was standing by the preserving pan all the while!"

The confectioner apologized humbly, and hurried away to bring out his best sweets for his irritable little customer. Sir Buzz chose about a hundredweight of them, and said, "Quick, tie

them up in something and give them into my hand; I'll carry them home."

"They will be a good weight, sir," smiled the confectioner.

"What business is that of yours, I should like to know?" snapped Sir Buzz. "Just you do as you're told, and here is your money." So saying he jingled the four shillings in his pocket.

"As you please, sir," replied the man cheerfully, and he tied up the sweets into a huge bundle, which he placed on the little manikin's outstretched hand. He fully expected him to sink under the weight, but with a *boom! bing!* he whizzed off with the money still in his pocket.

He alighted at a corn chandler's shop and, standing behind a basket of flour, called out at the top of his voice, "Ho! ho! Sir Chandler, bring me flour!"

And when the corn chandler looked round his shop and out of the window and down the street without seeing anybody, the one-span manikin with his beard trailing on the ground cried again louder than before, "Ho! ho! Sir Chandler, bring me flour!"

Then, on receiving no answer, he flew into a violent rage, and ran and bit the unfortunate corn chandler on the leg, pinched him, and kicked him, saying, "Impudent varlet! Don't pretend you couldn't see me! I was standing close beside you, behind that basket!"

So the corn chandler apologized humbly for his mistake, and asked Sir Buzz how much flour he wanted.

"Two hundredweight," replied the manikin, "two hundredweight, neither more nor less. Tie it up in a bundle, and I'll take it with me."

"Your honor has a cart or beast of burden with you, doubtless?" said the chandler. "Two hundredweight is a heavy load."

"What's that to you?" shrieked Sir Buzz, stamping his feet. "Isn't it enough if I pay for it?" And then he jingled the money in his pocket again.

So the corn chandler tied up the flour in a bundle and placed it in the manikin's outstretched hand, expecting it would crush him, when with a *whiz* Sir Buzz flew off, the shillings still in his pocket. *Boom! bing! boom!*

The soldier's son was just wondering what had become of his one-span servant when the little fellow alighted beside him. Wiping his face with his handkerchief, as if he were dreadfully hot and tired, he said thoughtfully, "Now I do hope I've brought enough. You men have such terrible appetites!"

"More than enough, I should say," laughed the lad, looking at the huge bundles.

Sir Buzz cooked some griddle cakes, and the soldier's son ate three of them and a handful of sweets. But the one-span manikin gobbled up the rest, saying at each mouthful, "You men have such terrible appetites—such terrible appetites!"

After that, the soldier's son and his servant Sir Buzz traveled many miles until they came to the king's city. This king had a daughter called Princess Blossom, who was so lovely, and tender, and slim, and fair, that she weighed only as much as

five flowers. Every morning she was weighed on golden scales and the scales always turned when the fifth flower was added, neither less nor more.

Now it so happened one day that the soldier's son by chance caught a glimpse of the lovely, tender, slim and fair Princess Blossom, and fell desperately in love with her. He would neither sleep nor eat his dinner, and did nothing all day but say to his faithful manikin, "Oh, dearest Sir Buzz! Oh, kind Sir Buzz! Carry me to the Princess Blossom that I may see and speak to her."

"Carry you!" snapped the little fellow, "That's a likely story! Why, you're ten times as big as I am. You should carry *me!*"

Nevertheless, the soldier's son begged and prayed, grew pale and pined away with thinking of Princess Blossom. Sir Buzz, who had a kind heart, was moved and bade the lad sit on his hand. Then with a tremendous *boom! bing! boom!* they whizzed away and were in the palace in a second.

Since it was nighttime, the Princess was asleep.

The booming wakened her and she was frightened to see a handsome young man kneeling beside her. She began to scream, but stopped when the soldier's son, in the most elegant language and with great politeness, begged her not to be alarmed. After that they talked together about everything delightful, while Sir Buzz stood at the door as sentry. He placed a brick in the doorway so that he might not seem to pry upon the young people.

When dawn was just breaking, the soldier's son and Princess Blossom, wearied of talking, fell asleep. Thereupon Sir Buzz, being a faithful servant, asked himself, "Now what is to be done? If my master remains here asleep, someone will discover him, and he will be killed as sure as my name is Buzz. But if I wake him, ten to one he will refuse to leave."

So without more ado he put his hand under the bed, and *bing! boom!* carried it into a large garden outside the town. There he set it down in the shade of the biggest tree. Pulling up the next biggest tree by the roots, he threw it over his shoulder, and marched up and down keeping guard.

Before long the whole town was in commotion, because the Princess Blossom had been carried off, and all the world and his wife turned out to look for her. By and by the one-eyed Chief Constable came to the garden gate.

"What do you want here?" cried valiant Sir Buzz, making passes at him with the tree.

The Chief Constable with his one eye could see nothing save the branches, but he replied sturdily, "I want the Princess Blossom!"

"I'll blossom you! Get out of *my* garden, will you?" shrieked the one-span manikin, with his one-and-a-quarter-span beard trailing on the ground. With that he belabored the Constable's pony so hard with the tree that the pony bolted away, nearly throwing its rider.

The poor man went straight to the king, saying, "Your Majesty! I am convinced Your Majesty's daughter, the Princess Blossom, is in Your Maj-

esty's garden, just outside the town, as there is a tree there which fights terribly."

Upon this the king summoned all his horses and men, and going to the garden tried to get in. But Sir Buzz behind the tree routed them all. The noise of the battle, however, awoke the young couple, and as they were now convinced they could no longer exist apart, they determined to fly together. So when the fight was over, the soldier's son, the Princess Blossom, and Sir Buzz set out to see the world.

The soldier's son was so enchanted with his good luck in winning the Princess that he said to Sir Buzz, "My fortune is made already. I shan't want you any more. You can go back to your mistress."

"Pooh!" said Sir Buzz. "Young people always think so. However, have it your own way. Only take this hair out of my beard, and if you *should* get into trouble, burn it in the fire. I'll come to your aid."

Sir Buzz boomed off, and the soldier's son and

the Princess Blossom lived and traveled together very happily, until at last they lost their way in the forest, and wandered about for some time without food. When they were near to starvation, a Brahman found them, and hearing their story said, "Alas! You poor children! Come home with me and I will give you food."

Now had he said, "I will eat you," it would have been nearer the truth, for he was no Brahman but a dreadful vampire who loved to devour handsome young men and slender girls. Knowing none of this, the couple went with him quite cheerfully. He was most polite, and when they arrived at his house, he said, "Please get ready whatever you want to eat, for I have no cook. Here are my keys; open any cupboards save the one with the golden key. I will go and gather firewood."

While Princess Blossom prepared the meal, the soldier's son opened all the cupboards. In them he found lovely jewels, and dresses, and cups and platters, and such bags of gold and silver that his curiosity got the better of his discretion. Disregarding the Brahman's warning, he said, "I *will* see what wonderful thing is hidden in the cupboard with the golden key." So he opened it, and lo! it was full of human skulls, picked quite clean, and beautifully polished. At this dreadful sight the soldier's son flew back to the Princess Blossom, and cried, "We are lost! We are lost! This is no Brahman, but a horrid vampire."

At that moment they heard him at the door, and the Princess, who was brave and kept her wits about her, barely had time to thrust the magic hair into the fire before the vampire, with his sharp teeth and fierce eyes, appeared.

At the selfsame moment *boom! boom! bing!* was heard, coming nearer and nearer.

The vampire, who knew very well who his enemy was, changed into a heavy rain pouring down in torrents, hoping thus to drown Sir Buzz, but *he* changed into the storm wind beating back the rain. Then the vampire changed into a dove,

but Sir Buzz, pursuing it as a hawk, pressed it so hard that it barely had time to change into a rose and drop into King Indra's lap as he sat in his celestial court listening to the singing of his dancing girls. Sir Buzz, quick as thought, changed into an old musician, and standing beside the bard who was thrumming the guitar, said, "Brother, you are tired; let *me* play."

He played so wonderfully, and sang with such sweetness, that King Indra said, "What shall I give you as a reward? Name what you please, and it shall be yours."

Sir Buzz replied, "I ask only the rose that is in Your Majesty's lap."

"I had rather you asked more, or less," said King Indra. "It is but a rose, yet it fell from heaven. Nevertheless, it is yours."

So saying, he threw the rose toward the musician, and lo! the petals fell in a shower on the ground. Sir Buzz went down on his knees and instantly gathered them up. But one petal escaped, and changed into a mouse. Thereupon Sir Buzz, with the speed of lightning, turned into a cat which caught and gobbled up the mouse.

All this while the Princess Blossom and the soldier's son, shivering and shaking, were awaiting the issue of the combat in the vampire's hut. Suddenly they heard a *bing! boom!* as Sir Buzz arrived, victorious, shook his head, and said, "You two had better go home, for you are not fit to take care of yourselves."

Sir Buzz gathered together the jewels and gold in one hand, placed the Princess and the soldier's son in the other, and whizzed away home where the lad's poor mother, who all this time had been living on the two shillings, was delighted to see them.

With a louder *boom! bing! boom!* than usual, Sir Buzz, without even waiting for thanks, whizzed out of sight, and was never seen or heard of again.

But the soldier's son and the Princess Blossom lived happily ever after.

The Tiger, the Brahman, and the Jackal

ONCE UPON A TIME, a tiger was caught in a trap. He tried in vain to get out through the bars, and rolled and bit with rage and grief when he failed.

By chance a poor Brahman came by.

"Let me out of this cage, O pious one!" cried the tiger.

"Nay, my friend," replied the Brahman mildly, "you would probably eat me if I did."

"Not at all!" swore the tiger with many oaths. "On the contrary, I should be forever grateful, and serve you as a slave!"

When the tiger sobbed and sighed and wept and swore, the pious Brahman's heart softened, and at last he consented to open the door of the cage. Out popped the tiger and, seizing the poor man, cried, "What a fool you are! What is to prevent my eating you now? After being cooped up so long I am terribly hungry!"

The Brahman pleaded loudly for his life. At first the tiger ignored his pleas, but then the beast promised to let the Brahman go if the man could find three things that thought the tiger's action unjust.

So the Brahman set out to find something to ask. He first asked a pipal tree what it thought of the matter, but the pipal tree replied coldly, "What have you to complain about? Don't I give shade and shelter to everyone who passes by, and don't they in return tear down my branches to feed their cattle? Don't whimper — be a man!"

Then the Brahman, sad at heart, went farther afield till he saw a buffalo turning a well-wheel. But he fared no better from it, for it answered, "You are a fool to expect gratitude! Look at me! While I gave milk they fed me on cottonseed and oil cake, but now I am dry they yoke me here, and give me refuse as fodder!"

The Brahman sadly asked the road to give him its opinion.

"My dear sir," said the road, "how foolish you are to expect anything else! Here am I, useful to everybody, yet all, rich and poor, great and small, trample on me as they go past, giving me nothing but the ashes of their pipes and the husks of their grain!"

At this the Brahman turned back sorrowfully. On the way he met a jackal who called out, "Why, what's the matter, Mr. Brahman? You look as miserable as a fish out of water!"

The Brahman told him all that had occurred. "How very confusing!" said the jackal when the recital was ended. "Would you mind telling me over again, for everything has got so mixed up?"

The Brahman told it all over again, but the jackal shook his head in a distracted sort of way and still could not understand.

"It's very odd," said he, sadly, "but it all seems to go in at one ear and out at the other! I will go to the place where it all happened, and then perhaps I shall be able to give a judgment." So they returned to the cage, where the tiger was waiting for the Brahman, sharpening his teeth and claws.

"You've been away a long time!" growled the savage beast. "But now let us begin our dinner."

"*Our* dinner!" thought the wretched Brahman, his knees knocking together with fright. "What a remarkably delicate way of putting it!"

"Give me five minutes, my lord!" he pleaded, "in order that I may explain matters to the jackal here, who is somewhat slow in his wits."

The tiger consented, and the Brahman began the whole story over again, not missing a single detail, and spinning as long a yarn as possible.

"Oh, my poor brain! Oh, my poor brain!" cried the jackal, wringing his paws. "Let me see! How did it all begin? You were in the cage, and the tiger came walking by—"

"Pooh!" interrupted the tiger, "What a fool you are! *I* was in the cage."

"Of course!" cried the jackal, pretending to tremble with fright. "Yes! I was in the cage — no I wasn't — dear! dear! where are my wits? Let me see — the tiger was in the Brahman, and the cage came walking by — no, that's not it, either! Well, don't mind me, but begin your dinner, for I shall never understand!"

"Yes, you shall!" returned the tiger, in a rage at the jackal's stupidity. "I'll *make* you understand! Look here — I am the tiger —"

"Yes, my lord!"

"And that is the Brahman —"

"Yes, my lord!"

"And that is the cage—"

"Yes, my lord!"

"And I was in the cage—do you understand?"

"Yes — no — please, my lord —"

"Well?" cried the tiger impatiently.

"Please, my lord! How did you get in?"

"How! Why in the usual way, of course!"

"Oh, dear me! My head is beginning to whirl again! Please don't be angry, my lord, but what is the usual way?"

At this the tiger lost patience and, jumping into the cage, cried, "This way! Now do you understand how it was?"

"Perfectly!" grinned the jackal, as he dexterously shut the door. "And if you will permit me to say so, I think matters will remain as they were!"

The Banyan Deer

THERE WAS ONCE A DEER the color of gold.
His eyes were like round jewels, his horns were
white as silver, his mouth was red like a flower, his
hoofs were bright and hard. He had a large body
and a fine tail.

He lived in a forest and was king of a herd of
five hundred Banyan Deer. Nearby lived another
herd of deer, called the Monkey Deer. They too
had a king.

The king of that country was fond of hunting
the deer and eating deer meat. He did not like to
go alone so he called the people of his town to go
with him, day after day.

The townspeople did not like this, for while
they were gone no one did their work. So they
decided to make a park and drive the deer into it.
Then the king could go into the park and hunt

and they could go on with their daily work.

They made a park, planted grass in it and provided water for the deer, built a fence around it, and drove the deer into it. Then they shut the gate and went to the king to tell him that in the park nearby he could find all the deer he wanted.

The king went at once to look at the deer. First he saw the two deer kings, and granted them their lives. Then he looked at their great herds.

Some days the king would go to hunt the deer, sometimes his cook would go. As soon as any of the deer saw them they would shake with fear and run. But when they had been hit once or twice they would drop down dead.

The king of the Banyan Deer sent for the king of the Monkey Deer and said, "Friend, many of the deer are being killed. Many are wounded besides those who are killed. After this, suppose one from my herd goes up to be killed one day, and the next day let one from your herd go up. Fewer deer will be lost this way."

The Monkey Deer agreed. Each day the deer whose turn it was would go and lie down, placing its head on the block. The cook would come and carry off the one he found lying there.

One day the lot fell to a mother deer who had a young baby. She went to her king and said, "O King of the Monkey Deer, let the turn pass me by until my baby is old enough to get along without me. Then I will go and put my head on the block."

But the king did not help her. He told her that if the lot had fallen to her she must die.

Then she went to the king of the Banyan Deer and asked him to save her.

"Go back to your herd. I will go in your place," said he.

The next day the cook found the king of the Banyan Deer lying with his head on the block. The cook went to the king, who came himself to find out about this.

"King of the Banyan Deer! Did I not grant you your life? Why are you lying here?"

"O great King!" said the king of the Banyan Deer. "A mother came with her young baby and told me that the lot had fallen to her. I could not ask anyone else to take her place, so I came myself."

"King of the Banyan Deer! I never saw such kindness and mercy. Rise up. I grant your life and hers. Nor will I hunt the deer any more in either park or forest."

Favorite Fairy Tales
Retold by
Virginia Haviland